THE
TERRORIST
OF
PROVIDENCE
STREET

ALSO BY STEPHEN MORAN

ELLA

© 2016 Stephen John Moran

ISBN: 0692711953

ISBN-13: 978-0692711958

THE
TERRORIST
OF
PROVIDENCE
STREET

STEPHEN MORAN

MORAN PUBLISHING
LAS VEGAS, NEVADA

ACKNOWLEDGEMENTS

This collection of stories was a long time in the making and truly took a team to pull a finished book from the tattered mess of drafts that I stitched into a manuscript. The stories span the years and the miles of my writing life and with help of the editors, artists, and designers that worked on this book – it came together in a way I simply couldn't have accomplished on my own. I am indebted to you all.

THE TEAM

Marielle van Broekhoven
Cover Artist

S. A. Joo
Editor

Jette Harris
Editor

Jessica Wynn
Cover Designer

Sean Hoade
Interior Design

Ann Hoade
Proofreader

This collection is dedicated to my writing mentor. He challenged me to write about the things that keep us awake at night.

Edgardo Vega Yunqué
May 20, 1936 – August 26, 2008

TAN, WITH BROWN EYES

Scott sat in a daze for some minutes, letting time flow over him in a steady waste. His food was untouched on his plate, the gravy getting cold. Co-workers bustled about, but he ignored them. Dishes were being washed, floors were being swept, and customers were being served; all in a day's work. Someone called his name, but he did not turn. The voice continued, insistent, almost angry.

"How come you didn't send me a story this week?" Melissa asked.

Scott looked at her, wondering if he should answer. She painted a picture of torture with crossed, golden arms and readied impatience. Dark beauty with burning eyes—oh, so far away. He closed his eyes while the picture remained. He reached without opening his eyes and drew her closer toward him. Her skin felt smooth under his touch.

"I'm sorry." He ran his fingers along her arm.

"Be sure to send it next week, okay?" She tried to turn away, but he held her arm and pulled her closer.

"Melissa ..." he tried to speak, but nerves cut his voice away, leaving scraps of thoughts unsaid.

"What is it, Scott?" She remained in his grasp, not fighting and letting him run his fingers over arms, cheeks, and golden skin.

One moment, another, and time ran on forever. His mind faded into her beauty and he wished for one damn time to kiss her.

"Nothing," he said. He released her from his grip and returned to staring at his mashed potatoes.

Shaking her head, she walked away.

The evening shift passed as if it didn't exist. Take orders, run food, wipe tables, count money. An endless haze of eternal tedium. On and on, the night bled monotony, only broken by seeing her, touching her, thinking of her. *How can she be so close yet so far away?*

At home, alone and strangled by images of Melissa, he turned on the television. The faces and sounds did not reach his eyes or ears as he concentrated on thoughts of her. He took one of his notebooks from the desk and placed it next to him, hoping, or rather, wishing to write. He flipped the pages, turning to the last one. The month at the top read *April*.

I haven't written in my journal in four months. He looked at the last entry, knowing the words by memory:

> I don't think one can fool with fantasy forever. There comes a time in every man's life that one must be realistic and face the facts. The years pass as I do nothing and say nothing. I see them all move on, leaving me behind to record the futility. I might indeed fade away completely if not for her. Solitude and melancholy can't erase my thoughts of her. I wonder if she truly knows that I exist.

He shut the journal and winced. Covering his eyes with his hands, he blocked out images from the television and concentrated on a perfect vision of Melissa in his mind—her walking, smiling, talking, turning her head to look at him over her shoulder, shiny, bright eyes, filled with laughter. Watching her work, setting trays and running food, busing plates and wiping counters. Heaven each night; hell every shift.

The phone rang, ending his reverie. He let it ring and ring, not caring to talk with anyone. Instead, he threw the notebook on the floor and closed his eyes, waiting for sleep.

* * *

While getting ready for work the following week, he obsessed over his lack of courage. The story she requested remained on his desk and he eyed it as he dressed.

"I will give this to her tonight." He folded the paper and placed it inside his apron.

At work, he waited with impatience for Melissa to arrive. *This will be the night.* He repeated it over and over.

She arrived a few minutes late for the dinner shift, an unusual occurrence. Waiting near the employee table, he wanted a small amount of time to speak with her. She was delayed getting to him, talking with co-workers and customers, and checking herself in the mirror as she walked past. When she drew near, he felt sweat on his forehead and a stunning emptiness in his mind.

"Hello, Scott." She smiled and leaned on the table, which sent a shimmer of nervous energy down his spine.

"Hi. How are you?"

"Okay, I guess."

"Just okay? What's wrong?"

She sighed and paused, re-tying her apron. "Trouble in Boyfriend Land."

Scott tried to say something, but couldn't. His tongue felt thick and useless.

She answered the question before he asked, "Yes, we're back together."

The words cut the space between them and ripped his stomach like hot coals.

"Well, as long as you're happy." He walked into the break area. He lit a cigarette and leaned against the wall, thoughts of flying monkeys in his head.

He avoided her for the rest of the shift, pretending to be busy. Often, he muttered to himself and cursed the folded paper in his apron. He rushed through end-of-shift duties—wanting to get back to his apartment—wanting to be alone. She approached him while he counted his money.

"Are you going to the bar?" she asked.

"I don't think so."

Her arm brushed against him, sending a tremor over his body. "Please go. Just for one drink."

He sighed again. *I can't say no to her.* "I don't know. I have to get some writing done."

"On a Friday night? Give me a break. Promise you'll be there for a drink."

"One drink," he said.

Scott sipped a beer and waited for Melissa, silent while his co-workers talked. His eyes remained on the door, watching for her. A voice asked him a question, but he ignored it. Finishing his beer, Scott lifted the empty glass, and the bartender slid a full, frosty mug to him.

"That's a neat trick." Scott tossed a tip on the bar.

"Thanks," the bartender answered, ringing a bell and tossing the tip into a large ceramic vase.

As promised, she arrived at last call for one drink. She came over to him, smiling widely, and placed a hand upon his shoulder.

"I'm glad you're here. I knew you wouldn't let me down."

"Happy to be of service." Scott gulped the beer to find courage and lit a cigarette to calm his nerves.

She sat next to him and ordered a drink. Content to enjoy being close to her, he was silent while she talked with co-workers about the evening shift, trips to the mall, and the stress of being a mother.

Turning from the others, she focused her dark, brown eyes upon him. "So," she began, "What's up?"

"Nothing."

"You still didn't send me the story you promised."

"I know. I will. Don't worry," he said. Someone next to her began talking about a wedding, catching her attention.

The music played, people talked, and the bartender washed glasses. Scott scanned the bar, wondering what thoughts others might be harboring. *I bet the bartender wants us to leave.* He finished his beer, paid the bill, and slid off the bar stool. Approaching the door, he glanced over a shoulder to be sure Melissa was following him.

In the parking lot, the workers stood around talking. He huddled by Melissa's side silently and listened to her talk of baby showers, cheating boyfriends, fad diets, and many other things of which he had no opinion. The conversation wound down, and Melissa made her way toward her car. Scott followed behind her, knowing it was his chance to speak. She leaned on her car, waiting, and smiled at him.

"What are you thinking?" she asked.

"About a story."

"That's what you always say." she laughed.

"It's usually the case." He moved closer and reached his arms around her, pulling her against his chest. "I'm glad I didn't go home." He rubbed his hand over her back and shoulders, knowing she was in his arms, even if only for a moment.

"I'm glad for that too," she said.

"You're wonderful, Melissa. Never forget that."

"Oh, stop it."

He fell silent, wanting the sensation of having her close to linger. She tried to pull away, but he held her a moment longer.

"Close your eyes."

"Why?"

"Just because." Still holding her against him, he smiled.

He leaned down and kissed her on the cheek. After kissing her once more, lightly on the lips, he reached into his apron and placed the folded pieces of paper into her hand.

KARL MARX: A REFUTATION

The rumor that Paul, the general manager, hired a monkey to be a server persisted all week. Not one employee could verify the fact or had seen a monkey in the restaurant.

Paul deflected the questions and merely stated, "Karl starts on Friday."

He refused to give further details, which led to much speculation. Some wondered if Paul hired a real-life monkey or was making some sort of statement about the general quality of new hires in recent months.

Scott arrived early for his shift that Friday night, not wanting to miss the arrival of the monkey, Karl. He placed his bag on the employee bench and went to make himself coffee. A few workers stood around the coffee station, chatting and enjoying the free time before the dinner rush. Kim rambled on as usual, with the others listening with less than perfect attention.

"I wonder if Karl has restaurant experience," Kim said.

Scott remained silent and eyed her as she ran her fingers through her thick, blonde hair.

"A monkey in a restaurant?" Dave asked.

Scott smiled at Melissa. She smiled back at him, transfixing his attention with full lips and pretty brown eyes. He squeezed her arm, running his fingers over her smooth tan skin.

"I think it has something to do with quotas," Scott joked. A few workers laughed, but sounded more nervous than amused.

"I don't want to work with a monkey," Kim said, shaking her hair back and forth in obvious displeasure.

The workers murmured their agreement.

"Why not?" a voice said.

"Huh?" Kim turned to answer.

A monkey stood in the doorway to the kitchen. He was a head taller than the countertop, which was approximately three feet in height. Waiting for a response with one foot tapping on the tile floor, the monkey picked at his teeth with a thick nail.

The blood red of the uniform stood out against his black fur and brown ears. He was ugliest monkey Scott ever laid eyes on. His eyes were set too deep into his skull, which gave him a sinister look when he smiled.

"I've never worked with a monkey," Kim managed to say.

"Sure, you have," Karl said, winking at her. The crowd around them laughed.

"I'm Kim." She extended her hand toward the monkey.

"Call me Karl—Karl Marx."

Scott blinked and looked around, but nobody seemed to think it was strange for a monkey to be named Karl Marx. He wondered if they knew while Karl Marx wrote *The Communist Manifesto*, his kids almost starved to death. He walked away with his coffee in hand as his co-workers questioned Karl. He heard laughter and turned in time to see the monkey pinch Kim on her backside. Scott shook his head and walked toward the side door.

He looked out, watching the cars passing on the highway, honking, and entering the parking lot. He sipped his coffee in silence as the sounds of laughter from his co-workers mixed with the sounds of traffic coming through the open windows. Feeling someone next to him, he turned and found Melissa close to him.

"It's odd," she said.

"What's that?" Scott put his arms around her and pulled her against him.

"Karl is a writer."

Scott thought for a moment. He rested his cheek against her forehead and sighed. His stomach felt tight and full of nerves. "What does he write?"

"He wrote a fantasy novel."

Scott kissed her cheek. "What can you expect from a monkey?" he laughed, feeling better.

Scott didn't see much of Karl during the monkey's first week of employment. During the first two shifts they worked together, Karl was surrounded by the female workers, who showered him with attention. Karl basked in the glow of his popularity; the fact that he liked to party after his evening shifts made him an instant success. Kim reported she spent a rather entertaining evening with him outside work.

"What do you mean, 'entertaining'?" Scott asked her.

"He's just a funny monkey, that's all." Secrets were hidden in her smile as she played with her hair.

Scott wanted to talk with Karl himself, but didn't get a chance until Monday afternoon. He sat at a table near the kitchen, eating a hamburger before his evening shift, when Karl walked in the front door. None of the other servers had arrived yet, and as there was nobody else to talk with, Karl made his way over to Scott. He hopped into the booth across from him and took a french fry off of Scott's plate. Scott stared at him, not amused. Karl smiled as he chewed and took yet another one.

"It's okay. I wasn't eating those," Scott said, not attempting to hide the contempt in his voice. Any desire to talk to this monkey about writing vanished.

"You don't like me, do you?" Karl asked him.

Scott didn't answer and grabbed the newspaper off the seat. He began to read, hoping Karl might leave him in peace to eat his meal.

"I hear you're a writer," Karl said.

Scott put down the paper and folded his hands across his lap. "Yes, I am."

"I wrote a novel myself."

"Congratulations."

"Thank you." Karl either didn't notice the sarcastic tone or chose to ignore it. "I want to be a best-seller one day like Stephen King, although I don't write horror. I write fantasy."

"Same difference."

"Really? What type of books do you write?" Karl asked, smiling once again.

Scott sighed and did not answer. *Do I have to get into this discussion with yet another writer?*

"Well?"

"I write literary fiction."

Karl whistled and clapped his hands together in excitement. "You're an elitist," he laughed.

"I write for myself without worrying about the issue of selling books," Scott said, feeling annoyed.

"An elitist," Karl insisted.

"As you wish."

"Don't you want to make money?" Karl asked him.

"I want to write what I feel in my heart. If that sells, so be it, but money isn't why I write."

"Liar!" Karl exclaimed, pointing his finger.

"It isn't always about the money."

"Yes, it is always about the money. All writers want to be on the best-sellers list and make loads of money. Some are just honest and admit it."

"I don't care about money."

"Liar!" Karl repeated.

Scott sighed again. He gripped his fingers together tightly. His fingertips changed from white to red from the pressure. "You're a capitalist pig."

"No, I'm a monkey," Karl laughed as he jumped down and walked into the kitchen.

Scott kept to himself that night, watching Karl flirt, joke, and clown his way through the shift. Karl was popular with the ladies and took liberties, groping nearly every female worker. Far from being reprimanded for such behavior, his popularity increased.

"This monkey does not work," Scott said to Tim, the shift manager.

Tim shrugged and pointed at Karl, who was chasing ladies around the kitchen with a towel in hand. He caught Kim and whacked her on the backside. Great fits of laughter broke out from the workers.

"He doesn't have time!" Tim walked away, shutting himself in the office.

Scott approached the food window. Food orders were stacked three plates deep, but Kris, whose job it was to place plates on trays, was preoccupied with Karl was rubbing her back. The monkey's hands moved down and rested on her ass.

"I have to set my own trays now, so you two can have more time to grope each other, is that it?" Scott said.

"You're just jealous." Karl stuck out his tongue.

Scott carried his food out into the dining room, kicking the door open with enough force to leave a scuff mark. When he returned, he saw Karl pushing himself against Melissa. Karl looked at him and laughed as his hands came to a rest on her shirt. He squeezed Melissa's breasts and jumped back, howling with laughter. His eyes remained on Scott.

"Hey!" Melissa laughed and shrugged.

Scott gnashed his teeth and took a step toward Karl. "You're disgusting."

"I don't see her complaining," the monkey responded.

Scott threw up his hands and went toward the back for a smoke. He lit a cigarette, taking a deep drag to settle his nerves. Slowly, he exhaled through his nose and took another drag. He leaned his head on his hand and sighed, rubbing his temples with his fingers.

"Don't let Karl bother you," he heard a voice say.

He looked up to see one of the cooks. "Hey, Dave."

Dave rubbed his hand on his shirt, which was soiled with food and grease, before he patted Scott on the shoulder. "The ones that count know."

"Thanks."

Dave lit a cigarette and sat down beside him.

"Karl is taunting me," Scott said.

"When?" Dave asked.

"Just now. With Melissa. I'm sure someone told him I have it bad for that girl."

Dave nodded and patted his shoulder again. "Don't worry. Melissa likes you."

Scott sighed and took a drag. He pushed his cigarette around, making patterns in the refuse of the ashtray.

"You should ask her out on a date," Dave said.

"Maybe ..." He snubbed his cigarette out and stood, fixing his apron before he returned to the front. He heard the servers talking about their plans after the shift.

"Are you going out tonight, Karl?" Kris asked.

Scott looked at her. Her hair was dark brown, which flowed over her shoulders, but she had pale skin and thin lips. *You can have the monkey.*

"Count on it," Karl said.

A cheer came from the workers.

"You can always count on Karl to party." Kim twirled her blonde hair between her fingers.

Scott ignored them and began counting his money in silence. They were making plans, and he wished to be invited. It'd been a few weeks since he was invited to join the workers for drinks.

"It's all about the writing," he muttered. He looked at his money, which was sixty-three dollars after a tip for the bartender, and shook his head. "I can't afford it anyway."

"Can't afford what?" Melissa asked.

"A drink."

"Come on. You can afford to have one drink. It won't kill you." She put her hand on his shoulder.

He smiled and squeezed her hand. "I have to write—"

"Nonsense. You can't say no to me. You're going out tonight, and that's all there is to it." She slapped his arm playfully as he pinched her side.

"Bad boy," she said, smiling. "Don't pinch my fat."

"For the last time, you're not fat," he answered. "You're beautiful, and you know it."

Smiling, she hugged him and kissed him on the cheek. "I'll see you there."

He squeezed her hand again before continuing toward the office.

* * *

Scott stopped at his apartment to shave and shower, which was why most of his co-workers were already at the bar when he arrived. He entered the front door and saw Kim, Kris, and others talking in a group. He waved to them, but his greeting was not returned. He walked by them to where Dave and Melissa sat and saw Dave's arm around her shoulders.

"Scott!" Dave extended his hand.

"Dave," he said, sitting next to him. He winked at Melissa as he signaled to the bartender.

"The usual?" the bartender asked.

"You remember?" Scott laughed. "You are a credit to the profession."

Scott lit a cigarette and surveyed the bar, which was packed with area workers after their night shifts.

"I got you a beer." Dave clapped Scott on the back and lit a cigarette of his own.

"Cheers." Scott raised he glass and gave Dave a nod.

"It's good to see you out again," Melissa said.

He reached over Dave and squeezed her hand. "I needed a break from writing."

Melissa smiled at him. Her pretty brown eyes were framed lightly with mascara. Her dark brown hair stuck to her forehead before she brushed it away. She leaned toward him and touched glasses, giving him a view of a black bra and beautifully tanned breasts. His eyes met hers, and he smiled again. The warmth spread in his stomach.

"I'm glad to be here," Scott said as Kylie, Dave's girl, walked in the front door.

Dave got off his stool and walked over to meet her, leaving Scott alone with Melissa.

"Tell me something," she said, taking Dave's stool. She smelled like flowers, and the touch of her arm against his made him feel dizzy. He wanted to say many things—how often he wrote about her, how often he imagined her naked, and her perfect golden skin next to his own—but couldn't.

"The novel isn't going well."

"I see." She leaned back on the stool and watched him.

She seemed disappointed, but Scott, with nerves in his stomach, concentrated more on his fingernails. He picked at them, peeling away his cuticles. "I'm writing about an outcast man and how society attempts to squelch individuality and personal freedom."

"Sounds fun."

Scott stared into his beer. He opened his mouth, but no sound came forth. *Tell her you love her,* he heard a voice say. He spun his head around but saw nothing. Returning his eyes to hers, words failed him and desperation spread in his veins. He ran a hand over his hair and took a deep breath. She remained quiet, waiting and watching him. Her eyes were intense, maybe a little angry.

"What do you want out of life?" he asked her.

She sipped at her drink with her eyes upon his. "I guess what everybody else wants: To be happy, secure, and to have a nice family," she said.

He nodded, but inside, he wanted to ask what she meant by being happy. *Don't ask that. Tell her you love her,* he heard the voice say again. He didn't look this time and drank his beer instead.

"What about you?" she asked.

"I want to be a published writer." He thought he'd captured it well with that statement and leaned back on his stool, crossing his arms.

"That's all?" She seemed confused and leaned toward him as if she hadn't heard him correctly.

"Nothing else will make me happy," he said flatly.

She shook her head, but didn't respond. She looked across the bar with her fingers clutching her glass, at a loss for words. Scott was about to speak, but a cheer from the workers stopped him.

"Karl!"

Scott seethed while the workers hugged and kissed. Their laughter rose over the music. Karl pushed through the crowd to the bar and nodded at Scott. He grinned and yelled for all to hear.

"Who wants a shot?"

A loud cheer came from the workers.

"I'll take one," Melissa yelled, getting up to join the others.

Dave took his seat once again with Kylie at his side. Without asking, Dave ordered shots from the bartender, which they drank off in silence. Scott closed his eyes but still heard the chorus of laughter from the workers. Karl danced on a table, kicking his furry legs high in the air. Scott groaned. The monkey executed a back flip, sending a roar of approval through the bar.

The bartender rang the bell and pushed a shot toward the monkey. "On the house!"

"He's a showboat." Scott's anger was palpable.

"Agreed," Dave said, lighting a cigarette.

"The damned monkey is a fantasy writer!" Scott said as if that statement explained it all. Eying Karl, he threw money on the bar before finishing his beer. Scott stood, put on his jacket, and took his keys from his pocket.

"Are you leaving?" Dave asked.

"I can't watch this." Karl was speaking with Melissa, and Scott wanted to put his fingers around the monkey's neck. He walked toward the door, ignoring Dave's farewell.

* * *

Later that night, Scott lay awake, deep in thought. He attempted to write in his journal, but after an hour of staring at nearly-blank, white paper, the one sentence he wrote displeased him:

> We must fight to retain our individuality in the face of attempts by society to homogenize its citizens into well-behaved lemmings.

Motionless, he stared at the ceiling. He resisted the urge to light a cigarette and continued to stare at the ceiling, making shapes of shadows cast by moonlight peeking at him through the blinds. Closing his eyes, his thoughts centered on the monkey.

"He is everything I'm not." Scott was shocked at how thin his voice sounded. He sighed and rolled onto his stomach, waiting for sleep.

* * *

Weeks passed without change. Karl remained popular, spending almost every night partying. Scott grew more bitter and angry as time passed, isolating himself from all social activity. His writing did not improve, and his efforts weren't helped by news that Karl's agent might sell his novel soon. The monkey informed him it was his first novel and that fact irritated Scott more than anything.

Scott arrived for his Friday shift to find the workers filled with excitement. The ladies were talking excitedly by the coffee station. He heard Karl's name and walked over.

"Karl gave his notice," Kim told him.

He's quitting? He felt a surge of joy and laughed. "Why?"

"Haven't you heard?"

Scott stared at her. He felt his heart skipping and his palms sweating. From the bottom of his soul, he wanted to scream, but instead, he attempted to gather himself. "I haven't worked the past couple of days. What happened?"

Kim clapped her hands together, as Karl often did, happy to inform him. "A publisher accepted Karl's book."

Scott blinked, his knees weak. "It can't be true. He finished that book less than six months ago. He couldn't have sold it this fast." The room seemed to dim, and Scott struggled to breathe. She continued to speak, but it took a few moments for him to focus on her words.

"He called to tell me," Kim said.

It all made sense and he was forced to lean on the counter for support. The room spun under his feet, and he felt cold—very cold. The floor rose to meet him until his cheek pressed against the tile, cool and comfortable against his skin.

Karl entered the kitchen to a cheer from the workers. He stood near the spot Scott lay prone on the floor, close enough for Scott to see the pink skin below his monkey fur. All the while, the co-workers chanted

Karl, Karl, Karl!

Scott heard their voices as if under water. He attempted to lift himself, but lacked the strength. His arm fell useless at his side. Looking up, he watched Melissa kiss Karl's cheek and her lips form the word "congratulations." Scott felt consciousness slipping at the sounds …

Karl, Karl, Karl!

TRANSITORY

The alarm chirped in Scott's ear, and he couldn't stop the incessant sound without rising, as he'd placed the clock on a table across the room. Dizziness swirled in his skull from the effort of getting out of bed. Smashing his hand down onto the alarm clock in anger, he entered the bathroom. Splashing water onto his face to clear the hangover from his mind, he was gripped by a wave of nausea.

Spinning the shower nozzle, he stepped under the light spray of water, without testing it. He screamed and almost fell out of the tub, frantically turning the knobs in an attempt to lower the temperature.

"The same routine, every goddamned day," he cursed aloud. He washed himself vigorously, shaking his head as he thought of how little time he had before work.

He left the shower in a rush, and as he dressed, he looked at the clock, which announced he had less than forty minutes until hell began again.

Sighing, he put on his work shoes and shut off all the appliances. He exited the apartment, thinking of the traffic he might encounter. As he left the building, a wave of heat pressed into his chest. The scalding midafternoon sun burned his skin as he jumped into his truck.

The air inside his truck seemed to be on fire, making it hard to breathe as he started the engine and immediately turned the air conditioning to its highest setting. Turning onto the street, Scott noticed that the major throughway was currently clear, but he shook his head, knowing that a parking lot's worth of vehicles awaited him a street away. Taking Main Street, which led to the highway, he could see the cars were backed up for a mile. Flipping on the radio, he wiped the sweat gathering on his forehead and settled into his seat, knowing the snarl of traffic ahead of him might take twenty or even thirty minutes to unwind.

He arrived with less than a minute to spare before his scheduled in-time. Running for the door, he pushed past a coworker he did not recognize in an attempt to clock in before being deemed late. The computer didn't cooperate with him, however, and gave an error message saying that he was not a scheduled employee. Scott squinted and made his way through the kitchen, seeing two more employees he did not recognize.

He knocked on the manager's door and waited, seeing a woman sitting at the desk who seemed to be entering information from a stack of papers into the computer. She turned towards the door after some moments and stood to let him into the office.

"Yes?" she asked, as if confused as to the reason for his presence.

He stammered briefly, trying to think of something to say. He knew her, but she was staring at him as if she had not seen him before.

"The computer didn't let me clock in. It said I wasn't scheduled," he finally managed.

"What is your name?" she asked, still not recognizing him.

"Scott Holden."

She offered a chair and he sat. He watched as she punched his name into the computer and waited as the machine whirred with effort, trying to find him.

The machine beeped, and his file appeared on the screen. She tapped the glass knowingly and wagged a finger at him.

"You are not scheduled tonight, as the computer told you already," she said, as if admonishing him for wasting her time.

"I wrote the schedule down last week. I know it's correct," he responded, anger rising within him.

She scrolled through his file, finding his schedule at the bottom.

"It says here you are not scheduled again until Sunday evening." She crossed her arms in finality.

"That can't be the case."

She simply pointed at the screen.

"The computer has spoken," she said. When she clicked the red X at the top of his file, his name disappeared from the screen. She returned to the business of entering the information from the papers next to the computer into the database. He let himself out of the office and mindlessly made his way towards his truck, passing unknown coworkers.

He watched television that evening but did not pay the least bit of attention to the programs. He couldn't comprehend what had happened in the afternoon. He always took great care in writing down the schedule the moment the managers posted it on Tuesday evenings. Had they changed it without telling him? Had they simply eliminated shifts perceived as unnecessary? Questions swirled through his mind.

He grabbed his cell phone and sent a text message to a coworker he sometimes shared a beer with after hours. Pacing the living room, he bit his nails as he waited for a response. His phone finally beeped, after what seemed an eternity, and he rushed to read the message.

"Who is this?" it said. He stared at the screen in confused horror, wondering if indeed he might be going crazy all in one day.

"This is Scott Holden."

He waited again, but the beep from his phone came much more quickly this time.

"I don't know you."

Closing his phone, he placed it on the coffee table. He sat with a thud on the couch and leaned his head back, staring at the ceiling.

"I don't know you," he repeated slowly.

***

The days that followed passed slowly in the heat of dead afternoons. Scott watched the endless traffic of people moving into and out of his apartment building, an occurrence so common that he watched with unseeing eyes as faceless neighbors hurriedly piled their meager possessions onto the back of rusted pickup trucks and scurried out of the city. He viewed an endless stream of movies rented from automated boxes he found to be at nearly every business around the city. He waited for Sunday evening. Needing the money, he hoped the shift might bring a lot of business. He fell asleep Saturday night with a bottle of whiskey next to him, thoughts of the week on his mind.

***

He woke to the sounds of his alarm, which ripped into the dead silence of his whiskey-induced sleep. With a groan, he rolled out of bed and slammed the alarm clock, feeling an intense throbbing in his head. He stumbled into the kitchen to force down a glass of water; intense dehydration gripped his body. He ignored the pain and made the journey to the shower, starting the water without being conscious of it. Stepping into the tub, he screamed as scalding water burned his skin. He cursed himself once again, hurriedly turning the knobs to change the temperature.

He dressed and took pain pills to dull the headache pounding at his brain. Pulling on his shoes, he shut off all the appliances and left the building. The heat of midafternoon slammed into his chest, taking his breath away. He walked quickly to his truck, the simple effort bringing beads of sweat to his forehead. He started the truck and blasted the air conditioning, the heat gripping his mind, erasing all save the need to cool his body.

Traffic was light for a Sunday. He left early enough to ensure he arrived on time for his shift. He didn't want management to have the smallest excuse to send him home. He turned onto the highway and was surprised to see very little traffic. He smiled and turned on the radio, finding a talk radio station.

"In the next segment, we'll discuss America's shrinking middle class and the rise of the part-time retail economy," the announcer said before the commercial break.

"What middle class?" Scott muttered as he pulled into the parking lot of his restaurant. He put on his apron as he approached the building and looked at his watch.

"Ten minutes early," he said, as he entered the building and made his way to the front, wanting to know in advance what section he had that evening. A tall young boy stood at the host desk. Scott didn't know him, and the boy stared with open hostility. Scott leaned around him and looked at the floor plan, trying in vain to find his name.

"What section do I have?" he asked the host, confused.

"Um, I don't know," the boy stammered. His face flushed a deep red. A server, a young girl wearing a plain black tee shirt and dark blue jeans, which seemed to be the uniform, approached him. He looked down uncomfortably at his own white shirt and black pants.

"Can I help you?" she asked. Her voice was filled with curiosity.

"I'm here for my shift tonight, and I can't find my name on the floor plan," Scott explained to her.

She eyed him carefully, looking over his uniform slowly.

"Are you sure you're in the right restaurant?"

"I'm quite sure. I've worked in this restaurant for over six months," he said with confidence.

She stared at him and said nothing in response to his statement. She simply turned from him and walked into the kitchen. A few moments later, a tall fat man holding a clipboard approached him, giving his work clothes the same confused once-over the server had.

The man extended a hand to him, which Scott shook. The tall fat man seemed friendly enough.

"Can I help you?" the man asked. "I'm Roger, the general manager for this store."

Scott stared at him, never having seen this man before now. He felt a sinking in his stomach and a tightening in his groin, as if he had to urinate suddenly.

"I was scheduled for work," Scott said.

"What is your name?" Roger asked. Scott told him and waited as Roger scanned his clipboard. "I'm sorry, but you are not on my list."

"That can't be," he said. "I was here on Wednesday, and the manager on duty showed me in the computer that I was scheduled for this shift, Sunday evening."

"Do you know the name of this manager?" Roger asked. His face showed his lack of belief.

"No."

Roger sighed and motioned for him to follow. He led the way through the kitchen, which seemed changed somehow from what Scott remembered seeing Wednesday night. Roger opened the office door and led Scott inside, offering him the seat next to the desk. Clicking the icon of the folder with the employee files, he typed Scott's name, both of them waiting with impatience while the machine whirred in effort.

After some time, the computer beeped and a message appeared on the screen:

NO MATCHING NAME FOUND IN DATABASE.

Scott stared in disbelief at the screen, his vision clouding for a moment as all of the facts of the day attempted to crowd into his brain. He felt physical pain in his head and placed his hands on his ears, as if to stop the entry of further stimuli.

"No, this can't be," he said.

Roger frowned and pointed at the screen.

"You are not in the computer. Therefore, you do not work here," Roger said, as if the logic in his statement was incontrovertible.

"I work here," Scott said, a weak attempt to disagree.

"You do not exist." Roger rose from the desk. He led Scott towards the exit at the rear of the kitchen, opening the door for him in silence.

The door opened onto an alley, and it took him some time to find his way to the main parking lot. He looked for his truck, but the spot he left it in was empty. He ran to and fro, looking in vain for his vehicle. In frustration he returned to the restaurant, hoping someone inside might have an answer to the riddle of his lost truck.

He opened the door but found nobody at the host desk. He ran from room to room, finding not a soul. Retracing his journey through the kitchen towards the manager's office, he pounded his fists on the door. He saw a small figure sitting at the computer. The person did not respond to his repeated assaults upon the door. Eventually, Scott stopped his pounding and simply waited, watching the figure type into the computer. After many minutes, the figure turned and yanked the door open.

A man stood before him, a small thin man with a receding hairline. He blinked at Scott with questioning eyes, as if waiting for him to explain his presence.

"Where is Roger?" Scott asked.

The thin man looked at him, his expression void of comprehension.

"There is no Roger here, boy," he said, his voice ripping into Scott's mind. He indeed wasn't sure if the man actually spoke or somehow was inside his head.

Scott turned, wanting to hear nothing further on this day. He ran for the exit and burst forth, screaming and waving his arms.

A MOMENT AND FOREVER

Scott arrived home late, but not so late it was unusual. Michael, the floor supervisor at the factory, delayed him a few minutes to offer him an extra shift on Saturday. Scott answered that he had plans with Diana. Offering an empty apology, Scott rushed home, hoping to catch her before bed.

Scott entered a dark, quiet apartment and paused for a moment in the doorway, unsure how to proceed. Usually when Diana went to bed before he got home, she left a light on in the kitchen and a plate of food on the counter. He flicked on the light and found an empty counter. He continued to the bedroom, opening the door slowly. The bed was empty, left as he made it that morning. He returned to the kitchen, looking for a note or some sign explaining the empty, dark apartment. The light blinked on the answering machine, so he pressed the button.

It was Diana. She needed to attend a retirement party for one of her bosses. She promised not to be late, but gave no definitive time frame. The machine stamped the time of the call at a few minutes before nine o'clock. The microwave clock showed midnight; he expected her return quite soon.

"I'll wait on dinner," he muttered, getting a beer out of the refrigerator and heading into the living room. He took a seat in the armchair, turned on the television, and put his feet up on the stool.

An hour passed without a call or arrival. Scott drank through the better part of a six-pack of beer, pulling the tabs off as he pushed each empty can aside. Constant glances at the clock failed to calm his nerves and he began chewing at his fingernails. Anxiety formed a physical presence in the bottom of his stomach, a knot hardening by the minute. He wiped sweat from his brow and checked the clock again.

The phone rang at 1:45, breaking the silent tension in the room. As his arm snatched the phone with an energy fueled by jealousy, he muttered a curse about acting like a schoolgirl.

"Hello?" He heard a roar of voices and music on the other end. The volume hurt his ears.

"Scott," Diana said, her voice slurred thick with alcohol.

Close to the phone, he heard a male voice urging Diana to hurry.

"Diana?'

"Yes, Scott. I'm going to party for a little while, okay? Don't wait up. I'll get a ride," she said in a blinded rush of words.

"Okay. I love you," he said, but she had already ended the call.

He opened the last beer, ripping the tab away and throwing it onto the floor. Shaking his head, he tried to understand her call and ward off the creeping thoughts of morbid jealousy. A question echoed in his mind: Where was she? Images of debauchery and treachery fluttered inside his brain.

Turning up the volume on the television, he attempted to drown the thoughts, the concerns, and the growing jealousy. He dug through memory, searching for a similar incident to quell his fears and enable him to sleep. However, no such memory came to his aid; Diana had always been punctual, habitual, *there*—always and forever *there* for him when he arrived home from work each night.

He sipped whiskey until his body drifted towards sleep. The last thing he saw before his eyes closed was the neon green numbers on the alarm clock: 3:15.

***

Darkness enveloped him, a darkness so complete it shrouded his path. Running and running to no place, sweat ran down his arms and cheeks. A babble of voices speaking foreign languages filled the air.

"It's an invasion!"

A woman screamed in the darkness, followed by peals of laughter, the echoes filling the space around him as if with light. The rumble of a train approached, coming fast and bearing down upon him, but he could not run. His feet felt trapped in shackles. A gong rang, and a voice screamed, a long terrible shriek that contained all his jealous anxiety. It came to a sudden halt.

"You are the dead!"

The train bore down. He felt the heat of the invisible lights burning into his back as he ran. The passengers engaged in an auction, selling his possessions.

"A book of stories, original. Do I hear one dollar?"

A mad demon's laughter ripped at his ears as he felt the train pushing against his legs.

"Not even a dollar!" the voice bellowed. A tremendous thunder of voices in all the languages of Earth answered in the negative.

"Burn it!" the crowd screamed in one voice.

A ripping sound shook his body and the train moved beyond him.

The alarm clock beeped an insistent chorus next to the bed.

He woke drenched in sweat and looked at the clock: 8:15. Diana's side of the bed remained empty. Jumping up, he checked the machine, but there were no messages. He checked the living room, half expecting to see her on the couch, but there was nothing. Walking onto the porch, into the hot sun of early morning, he stared up at the sky. A neighbor lay prone on a lounge chair, absorbing the sun and smoking a cigarette.

"It's going to be a hot one, Scott. You should work on a tan. You're pale from sitting in that house all the time."

"I guess," he muttered.

The neighbor lifted the visor of his cap, exposing his blue eyes. He lay on the chair, awash in tanned health with his skin heavily oiled, the whites of his eyes stark against the deep color of his face.

"Pull yourself together, Scott," the neighbor said.

Scott nodded as he heard the phone ring. Running back into the house, he felt a flood of hope and a glimmer of happiness touching at his veins. He grabbed the receiver off the cradle.

"Scott?" It was Michael. "Can you work today?"

"No, I can't. I'm waiting for Diana. She didn't come home last night."

Silence answered him. Finally, Michael spoke, "Did you have the dream again, Scott?"

Scott mumbled and held the phone away for a moment. The clock ticked, the refrigerator wheezed, and he struggled to breathe. "Yes," he said.

"Scott?" Michael asked after a pause. "Still there?"

"Yes, Michael."

"She left three years ago, Scott."

He hung up the phone and leaned against the wall. A tear worked down his cheek. "I know," he said.

MY PET DRAGON

Scott walked down Main Street toward the library, pausing to look down the road that led to the old ball-fields where he played as a child: An artifact of childhood a short walk down an unkempt road. *Can I take that short stroll and turn back the years*? Pushing the thought away, he continued the last hundred yards to the small building with faded gray paint.

"It looks the same as it did thirty years ago," he muttered before pulling on the handle and entering the semi-darkness of the lobby.

Happy to be out of the early February cold, he hung his winter coat on the hooks near the door. Rubbing his hands together, he scanned the room, which contained a desk in front of him and several bookcases. Hushed whispers reached his ears, but he couldn't locate the source. In the room on the left, a table with books piled to one side occupied the center of the room. The shelves were pushed back a few feet to allow extra space. Scott tiptoed into the room and saw nine people, four mother-daughter pairings and the librarian.

His gaze moved beyond the librarian. Long, flowing brown hair with bangs cut low on the forehead filled his vision. He recognized the woman a moment before their eyes locked. Twenty years changed so much and nothing, and a sliver of memory from those high school days pressed into his mind. She smiled, eyes twinkling and pretty, like he remembered. Scott found the nerve to walk forward with hand extended as sweat formed on his palm. She pressed his hand and nodded—almost a half-bow.

"How have you been?" she asked.

He avoided the mother's question. Scott noticed a tallish, thin girl standing behind her, peeking with curiosity at the man talking to her mother. "Who might this beauty be? She looks just like you."

"This is Madison." Her eyes filled with pride and she caressed the child's head. "She wrote a book, too, so she is very excited for the reading. She talked about it all week."

"Mom, please," the girl pleaded, resuming her place behind her mother's shoulder.

"How long will you stay in town?"

"This is the first time I've been out of the house in a while. I'm trying to get my feet under me again." He looked around for the librarian, hoping for some official act or request to take him away.

The librarian, a stern woman with short, straight, brown hair, wearing a flower print dress and gray sweater, glided towards them as if she heard his thoughts. The lady clapped a few times to get the attention of the room and introduced Scott to the mothers and daughters of Millville.

Scott took the cue and sat at the table. Grabbing a copy of the book, he took a deep breath. He pressed the spine to prevent it from snapping closed and let the book lay open on the table. He began the story, *My Pet Dragon*.

> There once lived a man with a dragon for a pet. The dragon, named Champ by the man's son, spent his days inside the innermost room of the house. The man spent hours each day, from the time he awoke until dinner, in the room with the

dragon. The son wished to spend time with the dragon, but Mother said never to bother Father when he was doing his work in the room. Mother always said the word "work" with a disdain the child couldn't understand. He simply wished to spend time with Father and the dragon.

One night at dinner, with beagles yapping under the table for scraps and affection, the boy tugged at his father's sleeve.

"Daddy, can I tell you what I want for my birthday?"

"Of course, my son," Father replied, ruffling his son's hair and pushing his plate to the side.

"I want the dragon to be my pet. I've been a good boy. Ask Mother."

The man looked at his wife across the table. She scowled and gripped her plate.

"I've warned you about filling his head with this nonsense. Billy, there are no such things as dragons."

"Must you, in front of him?" The man said, his head drooping a little and with a sigh audible only to the boy.

The male beagle tilted his head and licked the man's hand. The man smiled in spite of the situation, gripping the dog's muzzle and rubbing his nose with affection.

"Mommy, dragons are real! I heard Champ roar the other day," the boy said.

"Enough!" his mother said as her knuckles turned white from gripping her knife. "Tell him."

"I can't, and I won't. Dragons are real. I'm sorry you lost your magic," Father said, his voice low and resigned.

"Yes, I want Champ for my birthday," the boy said, feeding the dog a piece of meat under the table.

Mother slapped his hand, not taking her eyes off the man. "There are no dragons," she said, taking time with each word and pounding a hand on the table to end the discussion.

Later, when Mother paid the television her mind, the boy used the opportunity to sneak down the hall toward the room. The boy had never been inside the room. Tonight, he resolved to open the door.

"I will see the dragon tonight," he whispered with glee.

Pressing himself against the wall, he inched a hand toward the knob, trying not to make a noise. He heard a low growl and a hard crunching sound. Eyes widening, he placed his hand on the knob.

"Stop!" Mother snapped, grabbing his shoulder and pulling him down the hall.

"Mommy!" the boy exclaimed.

"Dragons do not exist. Never go inside this room. Do you hear me?" she said, shaking his shoulders.

He began to cry, and tears poured down his face. She pressed his rosy cheek against her chest, rubbing his neck.

"Dragons are real, Mommy," he said.

"No, they are not."

The father emerged from the room. The boy attempted to look inside, but his mother shielded his eyes. Dogs yipped at their feet as Mother gave Father a cold stare that filled the air between them.

"I will not hear of this business again," she said, leading the boy down the hallway.

The mother settled the boy into bed and read him a story. Then she went into the kitchen and grabbed the phone.

"I can't take it anymore," she whispered into the mouthpiece.

"I believe in dragons," the boy said to himself. Hearing his mother in the other room, he slipped back through the door into his secret space.

Scott finished reading and the room was silent. The woman stared at him and held Madison tightly against her chest, as if trying to protect her. A few scattered and confused claps met him, but otherwise, no reaction beyond blank stares and opened mouths.

The woman pushed forward and threw a ten-dollar bill on the table. She grabbed a book and placed it in front of Scott. He signed it without inscription, or being able to look the woman or Madison in the eye.

"Thank you," he said and slid the book toward the child.

Madison grabbed the book and ran for the door. The woman remained, lingering at the table.

"I hope you can be happy, Scott. I know how hard it must be," she said, then walked away. She got a few feet before Scott responded.

"But do you believe in dragons?"

The woman didn't answer and followed her daughter out the front door, not looking back again.

The Terrorist

Scott walked south along Central Street, passing all the familiar houses that never seem to change, get painted, or age with the years. He stopped at the corner of Quaker Street and debated taking the long way home. He decided against it and continued along Central. Dried, dead leaves and the remains of a snow storm crunched underfoot as he made his way up the final hill before taking a right onto Providence Street.

Quickening his pace when home came into view, he avoided looking at the graveyard across the street. Bounding up the small slope of the front yard, he jumped the wall onto the driveway and opened the cellar door.

The kennels stood on the left. Food spilled over the bowls, and the water contained dust and dirt, a foul smell filling the area. Tracing a hand over the top of the first cage, his fingers came away covered in dust. He made for the stairs and climbed them slowly. The faded, wooden steps creaked, and a coffee can filled with rusted nails shook as he approached the door.

He opened the door wide until it thudded against the wall. In the living room, boxes and trash filled the space. A lone mattress without bedding occupied the center of the room. Next to the bed, there was an ashtray overflowing with crushed cigarettes. A television rested on the floor. He peeked into the kitchen, empty of furniture. He stopped at the first room on the left. A *Transformers* poster hung at an angle by a single tack, and broken Tonka trucks littered the floor. Scott closed the door, pressing his forehead again the wood.

He continued down the hall and came to the door. The last door on the left was his room. Turning the knob, he pushed the door open. There was a writing desk piled with papers and books against the far wall. Otherwise, the room was empty. He sat in the desk chair. Reaching under the monitor, he pressed the button and waited for the screen to come to life.

Clicking the mouse, he opened a file. He cracked his knuckles and placed his fingers on the keyboard.

"I believe in dragons."

* * *

A crashing sound woke Scott from his sleep. He opened his eyes to see the roof ripped from the house and a great, coal-black dragon towering above the ruins. The dragon seized him with the massive talons digging into his shoulders, and rose into the sky. The wind stung Scott's face while the dragon carried him with great speed over the surrounding towns.

"Slow down," Scott said to the dragon.

"As you wish," the dragon answered, coming to a stop mid-air before hurtling toward the ground. At the moment before impact, the dragon veered and flew over the next hill. Landing in a wide clearing, the dragon deposited Scott on the ground and took a position next to a great oak tree.

"What do you want?" Scott asked, taking several steps away from the dragon.

"What do you want is more like. And why bother running? If I wanted to kill you, you wouldn't be alive."

Scott shook his head and rubbed at his eyes. "Is this a dream?"

The dragon breathed fire at him, and Scott dove for cover. "Perhaps that will wake you."

"I'm awake. Now, tell me why you destroyed my house," Scott asked, standing once again.

"An accident. My apologies. I came into existence from your belief, and I am yours to command."

Taking a few steps toward the dragon, Scott ran a hand through his hair before taking a pack of cigarettes from his pocket. "You'll do anything I want?" Scott asked.

The dragon laughed and snorted smoke, "I have no moral clause."

Scott paced for a few minutes, smoking and pulling at his beard. He smoked the entire cigarette before he spoke again. "Burn Town Hall," he ordered.

The dragon laughed again and lowered a shoulder to allow Scott to climb on his back. Once Scott settled into position, the dragon launched them skyward, heading with much haste toward Main Street. Soon, Town Hall came into view. Scott noticed no signs of life in the parking lot or windows.

"Hold on," the dragon said as the building came into range.

Scott attempted to speak, but the dragon spit fire, bathing Town Hall in light. He held on as the assault continued, and the dragon hovered in the air to fire again and again on the defenseless building. Flames engulfed the second story within minutes. Scott smiled with satisfaction as the sirens began to wail.

"Burn it all!" Scott screamed in the air.

The dragon spun and sprayed fire in all directions, igniting the surrounding houses. The dragon put fire to every house in town. The growing chorus of sirens followed the fiery show.

Scott heard a gunshot. The dragon snatched the man who fired from the ground, snapping him in half. As the dragon lifted him away from the flaming wreckage of Town Hall, Scott realized he had been shot.

Scott's hand found the wound near his temple and clamped against the gushing blood. The dragon swooped toward the next target. Scott slipped and plummeted toward the ground. As he fell, blood streamed into the air from the wound.

"Peace," Scott said a moment before he crashed.

* * *

Chief of Police John Brown waited on the front steps, looking around in every direction. He stopped to make a small nod of greeting to each man and woman on the task force. Pressing a finger against his lips, Chief Brown placed a boot on the first of four concrete steps leading to the one-story ranch. A gunshot shattered the silence.

SWAT swarmed ahead of him and entered the house. He listened to their calls as they cleared each room. He followed down the hall to the master bedroom. Walking inside, he saw Scott's body at the desk, dead with a gunshot wound to the temple. The gun rested under the chair, a spent casing beside it.

"Damn it, we won't get to question him. Search the place," he said, taking a pipe from his pocket. With a deft hand, he packed the bowl and lit it.

He supervised the detectives, but did not once interrupt the proceedings. Chief Brown placed a callused index finger on an engraving along the handle of the pipe: *DH*. The initials of his grandfather, a policeman long ago. Did he ever encounter such a scene in this small town?

Two EMTs entered the room, arms loaded with medical bags and cases.

"It's a suicide," a detective commented. The EMTs checked for signs of life despite the pronouncement.

"What can you expect from a Holden?" Captain Brown said. "What can you expect from a coward who threw a firebomb into town Hall?" He puffed at the pipe and watched the medic examine the body.

The young man made eye contact. "How many died in the Town Hall explosion?"

"Four. Two officers, a dispatcher, and a janitor, that poor bastard. He wasn't even scheduled to work. Was just there picking up his paycheck." John puffed again on the pipe.

"How can you remain calm?" the medic asked.

"I don't know, you just do, or you lose your composure. It's not easy on days like today. That business at the Town Hall is the worst I've ever seen."

He wanted to say more, to speak about his grandfather and tradition and doing the job without letting emotion get the best of you, say *I've seen a few cops die. That's part of the job, kid*, but a commotion from the hallway interrupted him. Chief Brown followed the din of voices to from the basement. He took the stairs down two at a time, careful not to hit his head against the low wall over the landing.

The sea of cops parted to reveal a massive hole in the concrete foundation. Flashlights illuminated a tunnel. Chief Brown grabbed a lantern from a rookie and plunged into the opening.

He entered a small room shaped like a hobbit hole. Thrusting the lantern forward revealed three skeletons, one adult and two children, seated at a small table, arranged as if at a tea party. John panned the lantern around the small space, light touching bones and remains buried into the wall, cemented in time. Skeletons ringed the family seated at tea, eternal witnesses to the party.

His mouth fell open, and the pipe dropped to the dirt floor. Struggling to breathe, Chief Brown wanted to tear his eyes from the skeletons at tea time, but felt frozen to the ground. One of the children's hands reached towards a tiny cup on the table. The sparkling porcelain hovered out of the child's reach. How odd to see a clean cup in a room of filth and dust! He heard words in his mind, and they made him wretch. *He spent time in this room. He was having tea with the skeletons ...*

He clutched at the wall for support to keep from falling. Without making a sign that he noticed the loss of his favorite pipe, Chief Brown retraced his steps to the front door and left the house. Staggering down the slope of the front yard, he pulled the badge from his chest and tossed it on the ground. He didn't get into his service vehicle, but instead continued along Providence Street, ignoring the yells and screams of cops running after him, trying to make him stop.

BONUS CONTENT

READ A SAMPLE CHAPTER FROM THE UPCOMING MORAN PUBLISHING RELEASE, *PREFACE TO A SUICIDE.*

THE MEETING

I enter the office listed at the address printed on Agent Smith's business card at two o'clock. He waits in the lobby and greets me with a warm smile, shaking my hand and patting my back in a familiar way. He escorts me to an interview room with a long rectangular table and three chairs; I sit across from him and wait. Sweat tickles my brow, and I fight the urge to wipe it.

"Is it hot in here, or is it just me?" I say, attempting to laugh, but my voice fails me.

"Oh, the AC unit isn't working well. You know these downtown buildings, don't you, Ray?" He laughs, but the mirth doesn't reach his eyes.

Yes, Mr. Agent, I'm sure you're quite well aware how much research into downtown Providence went into the operation at Kennedy Plaza, but I'll be damned if I will voluntarily offer you any information. I can hear John's words in my mind and nod at Smith as if everyone knows such information.

"Can I offer you coffee or tea? Water, perhaps?"

"Whiskey, if you have it."

He places a file on the table between us and gives another warm smile. "I'll see what I can do."

Opening the file, he lines the table in front of me with pictures. All of them are from the day two months ago. Photos of the burned wreckage that was formerly a trolley car. Images of body bags, three, which he taps with his index finger for effect. The final picture, of her, he holds up for me to see.

"She was pretty. A pity she ... fell in with the wrong crowd."

I don't respond or move. The door opens, and a woman I believe to be the secretary places a glass in front of me.

"Whiskey, neat."

I nod thanks and gulp the drink. "Another, please."

"I have a few questions if you are ready."

"I can't imagine you have anything to ask that I haven't been asked a dozen times. Do your worst."

He laughs and pulls an ashtray from a drawer in the table. "A cigarette?"

"I have my own." Taking my pack from the pocket of my jeans, I light one and wait for the inquisition.

Special Agent Smith places a cigarette in the ashtray, unlit, and folds his hands together. "Was your wife having an affair with Ryan?"

The breath leaves my chest as if I had been punched. After dozens of interrogations, I didn't think he could ask me something I hadn't been asked in so many ways.

"Not to my knowledge."

"Because, I can't think of any other reason why she might follow him into such ... an operation. Without your knowledge and involvement, of course."

"Of course." The secretary enters with the whiskey bottle and leaves after placing it next to my glass. I take a drag and pour another drink.

Agent Smith shuffles through the papers in the file as if searching for something. He places another picture in front of me. It's a black-and-white photo of Ryan and Rose holding hands at dinner. It's a downtown Providence Italian restaurant I know quite well.

"You knew nothing of this?" he asks, lighting the cigarette from the ashtray and waiting for me to respond.

I take the photo in my hands and examine it. From what I can tell, it doesn't appear to be fake or doctored. Not that I'm an expert, but I doubt the agent needed to fabricate this evidence.

"Rose ... spent time with many other men."

"Yes, I'm aware." He returns to hunting through the thick file. "Ah, I remember."

Opening the drawer in the table again, he puts a thick notebook on the table. I close my eyes and count in my mind, trying to calm my nerves. *He knows everything.*

"At trial Ryan stated ... Let me read from the transcript here: 'I wrote *Dissident* during my freshman year at Brown University.'"

I can't speak or breathe and wait for him to open the notebook.

"That would mean Ryan wrote *Dissident* one year before the attack on Kennedy Plaza," he says, flipping the cover open and turning the notebook so the words face me. "Can you read the words below the title for me, please? Humor me."

The words indict me, and I can't move my eyes. I can recite every word from the manuscript without help, because I wrote it. But I won't say it. I'll follow John's advice. If this agent wants to arrest me, I won't help him put the nails in my coffin.

"I've never seen that book in my life. It's a forgery."

Agent Smith laughs and presses a button under the table. In moments, the secretary enters with two pieces of paper, each wrapped in plastic. "We had a handwriting analysis done. You are the author of *Dissident*, Ray. The question I have is—

why would your brother take credit? It's not like you made the bomb or detonated it. The evidence shows you had no involvement in the attack at Kennedy Plaza."

Where is he going with all this?

Sipping the whiskey, I wait for him to continue.

"Where were you that day? Where were you the moment the bomb detonated?"

A bell sounds, and the agent rises from his chair in a hurry. As he takes his leave from me, I hear a flurry of voices outside the room. I finish the drink and light another cigarette. Special Agent Smith reenters the room but does not sit at the table.

"You are free to go. Our interview shall continue another time."

"Excuse me? What happened? I'll find out, anyway, might as well give me your version of it."

"Your father's lawyers. Don't worry, a federal judge will sign off ..." he pauses when I rise. "You will soon find out."

He does plan to arrest me. John was right. Without wasting time on civilities, I leave and follow the hallway back to the parking garage. Riding the elevator with my eyes shut, I can't get the image of that photograph out of my mind. *Ryan and Rose.*

About the Author

STEPHEN JOHN MORAN lives in Las Vegas with his beautiful wife Maggie, daughter Kiana, two dogs and a cat. He is the author of many novels and short stories, with *Ella* being the first to see publication. Stephen enjoys reading, sports, and spending time with his family.

Follow the Characters on Twitter

@EllaThomas22 and @GeorgeinVegas

Read Ella's Journal at

StephenJohnMoran.com/ellas-journal

Follow the story at

StephenJohnMoran.com

For more information, contact

StephenJohnMoran@gmail.com